You go to school every day.

So does Patrick.

Maybe you ride on a schoolbus.

So does Patrick.

After school you play with your friends.

So does Patrick.

In fact, there's only one difference between you and Patrick.

But it is a *big* difference.

Patrick is a dinosaur. A *big* dinosaur.

Patrick's friends are dinosaurs, too.

So is his teacher.

So are his Mom and Dad.

What's it like to be a student in a school for dinosaurs?

That's what Dino School is all about!

Collect all the
Dino School books!

Dino School

3

BATTLE OF THE CLASS CLOWNS

Jacqueline A. Ball

Illustrated by David Schulz

HarperPaperbacks

A Division of HarperCollins*Publishers*

*For Joellyn Ausanka, as exceptional a copy
editor as she is a sister and friend.*

*Special thanks to Catherine Conant and
Maggie Earley for the super dinosaur jokes
and to Margaret Lavezzoli for her helpful
classroom insights.*

Harper Paperbacks   *A Division* of HarperCollins*Publishers*
10 East 53rd Street, New York, N.Y. 10022

Produced by Jacqueline A. Ball

Cover and interior design by Nancy Norton,
Norton & Company

First printing: November, 1990
Printed in the United States of America
HarperPaperbacks and colophon are trademarks of
HarperCollins*Publishers*
10   9   8   7   6   5   4   3   2

BATTLE OF THE CLASS CLOWNS

CHAPTER
1

The day at Dino School had barely started. Already Henry Ankylosaur wished it were over.

Henry's nickname was Hank. He had hard, tough skin, like armor. He was shaped like a tank. That's why his dino friends called him Hank the Tank.

Today they could have called him Hank the Crank.

He felt cranky and bored.

He was bored with school.

He was bored with life.

He was *really* bored with cursive writing.

That's what his third-grade class was learning today. Mrs. Diplodocus, Hank's teacher, stood at the front of the room. Everyone called her Mrs. D.

Mrs. D. had a very long neck. Today she wore four necklaces on it. The necklaces were strings of pink balls.

She made a big loopy capital D on the board.

Then she made a whole row of capital D's.

"Now *you* try," she told the class.

Hank twirled the spinner on his hat. The spinner went "spring!" when he flicked it.

He chewed on his pencil.

He tried to make a D like his teacher's.

It came out looking like a squashed watermelon with curls.

He tried again.

"That's uglier than a tyrannosaurus's toenail," he muttered.

Hank sighed. He couldn't seem to do anything right.

He made a big X through his work.

He stared at it for a moment. Then his face brightened.

He leaned across his desk to Patrick Apatosaurus.

"Hey, Patrick," he said. "Did you hear about the dinosaur who could write all the letters of the alphabet except one?"

Patrick smiled at Hank. He knew Hank was getting ready to make a joke. Hank was always making jokes and wisecracks. Patrick always laughed, even if the jokes weren't funny.

Patrick was the nicest dino in Mrs. D's class. And the biggest. He was almost as big as Mrs. D.

"No," he answered. "What about him?"

Hank leaned closer. "His X stinked!"

Patrick looked puzzled. "I don't get it."

"X-stinked," explained Spike Stegosaurus. He was Patrick's best friend, and the coolest dino in school. "You know, man, like extinct."

Patrick frowned. "I hate that word!"

Swish-thump. Swish-thump.

It was Mrs. D. She was tapping her tail.

That meant she wanted quiet.

"Boys," she said. "Especially you, Hank. *Must* we start the comedy so early?"

"But I can't do these," complained

Hank. He pointed at the D's on his paper. "I mean, I can't do D's. Ha, ha. Joke."

Spike groaned.

Mrs. D. snapped her long neck across the room. Her feet and body were still in the front of the room. But her head and neck were bent over Hank's desk.

She looked at the X on Hank's paper.

She gave him an understanding smile. Then she moved the rest of her body to his desk.

She made a neat capital D on his paper. "Like this," she said. "Just keep trying. It will come."

Hank picked up his pencil. He sighed again. "By then I'll be too old to care."

"Don't be silly," said Mrs. D.

"That's like telling a pterodactyl not to flap," said Spike.

"Right. Hank is always silly," said Sara Triceratops.

Mrs. D. went back to the board. "Here are some D names."

She wrote her own nickname. *Mrs. D.*

She wrote another name. *Diana.*

Diana Deinonychus was the smallest dino in the class.

"We should use a *small* d for her," Hank told Spike.

Diana heard him. She made a face.

Hank tapped Ty Triceratops on the shoulder. Ty was Sara's twin brother.

"Know what you call the smallest dinosaur?"

"I give up," said Ty.

"Dino-Mite!"

Ty burst out laughing. Over by the window, Sara and her best friend, Annette Anatosaurus, laughed, too.

When Sara laughed, the bows on her horns wiggled.

Swish-thump!

Patrick looked puzzled again. "I don't get that one, either," he whispered.

This time Ty explained. "A mite is a bug that's almost too small to see," he said softly. "So mite means really, really small."

"Oh," said Patrick. "I get it now! Dino-Mite! That's pretty funny, Hank!" Then he started laughing, too.

Annette nudged Diana. "Hey, Dino-Mite!" she said in a loud whisper.

Annette loved to tease.

Diana glared at Hank. "Thanks a lot, Hank," she hissed.

"You mean, 'Tanks a lot,'" corrected Hank. "Get it? Hank the Tank? Tanks a lot?"

Swish-thump! Swish-thump!

"All *right*, Hank! Please!" said Mrs. D. "You know, if you would spend a little more time paying attention and a little less time making jokes. . . ."

The door opened.

Ms. Brachiosaurus came in. She was the principal.

She called to someone behind her. "Come along, Sam."

The dinos tried to see past her into the hall. But they couldn't. She was too big.

"Good morning," Mrs. D. said to the principal. "Has our new student arrived?"

The dinos still didn't see anyone. Then a tiny dinosaur's head poked around the corner.

"Come in, come in!" said Mrs. D. "We don't bite."

"Speak for yourself," muttered Tyrannosaurus Rex. He was the class bully. He was one *bad* dinosaur.

A short dino stood next to the principal.

He was even smaller than Diana.

He was very skinny.

Hank snorted.

"What is this, *Revenge of the Nerdosaurs*?"

"Don't be mean," said Patrick.

"This is Sam," Ms. Brachiosaurus said. "Sam Saurornithoides."

"Saur who?" said Spike.

"Sore what?" said Ty.

"Sor—*ry*," exclaimed Maggie Megalosaurus. "That's too hard." She went back to what she had been doing: sneaking a piece of Crunchum bar from her lunch bag. Maggie loved to eat.

"It's *not* too hard," the new dino piped up. His voice was thin and high.

He said his name slowly.

"Sore—OR—Nith—Oy—Deez."

"Sore—OR—Nith—Oy—Deez," a few dinos repeated.

Mrs. D. was beaming.

"See?" she said. "Hard words are easy when you break them into little pieces. Good work, Sam."

"Maybe I'll break *him* into little pieces," mumbled Rex. "Little wimp."

Rex hated anyone who tried hard.

Ms. Brachiosaurus walked to the door. "I can see Sam is going to get along fine," she said as she left.

"Sam, I'll get you some books from the storeroom," said Mrs. D. "For now, why don't you sit back there."

She pointed to an empty desk near Hank and his friends.

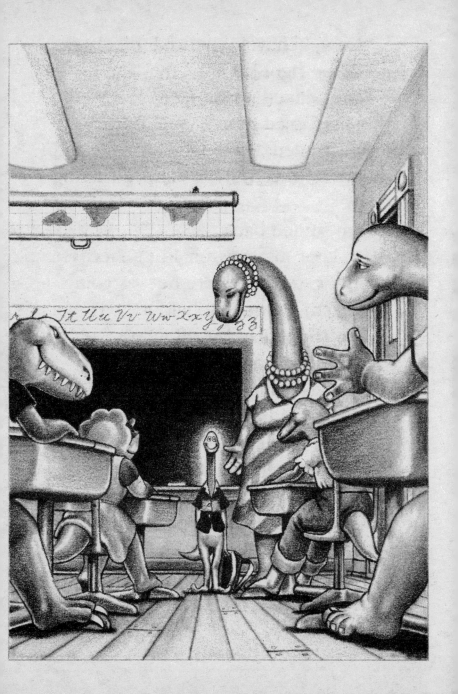

"Now, behave!" she told the class.

"I'll be right back."

Sam walked toward Hank. On the way he passed Rex.

Rex smiled. His smile was wide and nasty. It showed all his sharp, glittering teeth.

Sam smiled back.

He kept his eyes on Rex's face. He wasn't watching where he was going.

Rex stuck out a scaly foot.

Sam tripped and went flying.

He skidded on his knees.

"Bully!" Annette scolded Rex.

Patrick pulled the little dino up. "Are you all right?"

There were tears in Sam's eyes. His knees were scraped.

"Aw," said Sara. "You're going to have sores."

Sam gulped.

He wiped his eyes.

Then he smiled.

"Yeah," he said. "Dino-sores!"

The whole class sat quietly for a second. They were too surprised to do anything else.

Then Annette burst out laughing. So did Ty and Maggie. Then everyone joined in.

Almost everyone. Rex didn't laugh. He didn't have much of a sense of humor.

Hank didn't laugh, either. Who did this pipsqueak think he was? *Hank* made the jokes in Mrs. D.'s class.

"He's funny!" Maggie exclaimed. She held out her candy bar to Sam. "Have some chocolate. It will make you feel better."

Sam broke off a tiny piece. He began to nibble.

"How do you say your name again?" Annette asked Sam.

"Sore — OR — Nith — Oy — Deez," Sam answered. He said each part slowly.

Still munching on the candy, he sat down.

He was two desks away from Hank. He leaned back.

"But if my real name is too hard, you can call me Dino-Mite!" Sam said.

The class broke up. Even Rex laughed. Diana laughed louder than anyone. She was glad to get rid of the nickname herself.

"Hey, Hank," Annette teased. "Looks like you have some competition!"

Suddenly Hank felt sick. Everyone knew he was the funniest dino. He didn't want anyone else to tell jokes.

Patrick looked upset. "He shouldn't

be telling jokes," he said to Hank. "That's what *you* do!"

"Patrick's right," Sara agreed. She usually took sides with Patrick. She liked him a lot.

Besides, Hank was her friend. And he was there first. *He* should be the class clown.

Sara and Patrick both frowned at Sam.

Sam paid no attention. He sat back in his chair, wearing a big smile.

Mrs. D. came back into the room. She carried a stack of books. "What's all the monkey business?" she asked. "I heard you laughing way down the hall. Hank, are you at it again?"

"No," answered Ty. "It's the new kid. He's really a riot!"

Sara gave her brother a warning look. "He's not as funny as Hank."

"I don't think so either," agreed Patrick.

"Oh, I don't know," said Annette admiringly. "I think he's really *dino-mite!*"

Hank thumped the floor with his clubbed tail. He twirled his spinner.

This was not funny. Not funny at all.

CHAPTER
2

Hank was glad when recess came.

He couldn't wait to get outdoors.

He couldn't wait to get away from cursive writing.

He couldn't wait to get away from Sam!

Anyway, Hank always felt better after a game of Heads and Tailsies. He and Spike played every day.

The two of them got on opposite sides of the net.

Out of the corner of his eye, Hank could see Sam. He was with Ty and Annette and Maggie.

He said something. They all leaned down to hear better. Then everyone started laughing.

Hank clenched his fists. He swung his tail at the ball as hard as he could.

The ball flew way to the back of the field.

Spike raced back . . . back . . . . He made it! He got underneath the ball and turned around.

The ball bounced off his plates down to his tail. He smacked it back over the net.

Patrick and Sara clapped from the sidelines.

"Good one, Spike!" said Patrick.

"That was *really* fast running!" exclaimed Sara.

Hank bounced the ball off his head. "Know what you call a speeding dinosaur?" he called to them. "A pronto-saurus!"

Sara giggled. Patrick chuckled.

Hank felt much better. His friends *did* think he was funny after all!

He twirled around to face his audience.

"Which dinosaur rode with the Lone Ranger?" he called. "Tonto-saurus."

Spike grinned. Sara and Patrick jumped up and down laughing.

Hank felt terrific. He was still the champ. The king. The great Hank the Tank.

He knew tons of jokes. No one knew as many dino jokes as he did.

Spike returned the ball. Hank ran happily for it. He kept on talking.

"Okay, here's a good one! What do

you call the noises a sleeping stegosaurus makes?"

"We don't know!" called Patrick.

"Dino—" Hank began. But a high, thin voice cut in.

"Dino-snores!" the voice called out.

Hank looked behind him. There was that creepy little dino, Sam, looking smug. Annette and Ty and Maggie were laughing as if they'd never heard a funnier joke in their lives.

Some friends!

Hank wasn't watching the ball. It came down and hit him hard in the neck. He felt the wind get knocked out of him. He couldn't speak.

"Sorry, man," Spike said. "I didn't mean it."

Patrick and Sara came running. "Are you okay, Hank?" Sara asked.

Before Hank could catch his breath,

Rex came roaring up on his huge black bike. He was heading straight for them.

"Get out of the way!" Patrick yelled.

They all dived aside. Rex sped across the field.

As he passed the net, he reached out and ripped it down.

"Ha, ha," he shouted. "Game's over! You lose, you losers!"

The bell rang.

Spike shook his head. "That guy always wrecks everything."

Hank's breath was back.

Here was his chance.

He opened his mouth.

But he wasn't quick enough. Sam spoke first.

"That must be why he's called 'Tyrannosaurus Wrecks!' "

Hank gritted his teeth.

Patrick and Sara frowned at Sam.

The other dinos thought it was hilarious. They bounced up and down with laughter. They bounced so hard the ground shook.

Then they all swarmed around Sam and headed inside.

"Wait a minute!" Hank called. "What do you call a mean, ugly cowboy dino?"

The group paid no attention.

"Tyrannosaurus Tex," Hank finished weakly.

The group was gone.

"Oh, well," Hank said. He took off his hat. He pushed the spinner around very slowly.

"*We* think you're funny, Hank," said Sara loyally.

"Yes, we do," agreed Patrick. "Really funny."

"Then what's wrong with the others?" Hank asked.

"Oh, Ty always does the opposite from me," Sara said. "That's all. It probably has nothing to do with you."

"And everyone knows how Annette likes to tease," added Spike.

They walked toward the building.

Patrick had the net draped around his neck. It looked like a shawl.

Spike put the ball on his head. Then he shrugged his shoulders.

The ball bounced down the plates on his back. It was one of Spike's coolest tricks. Usually Hank loved to watch him. But today he barely noticed.

All he could think about was Sam, the new class clown. Sam, who was stealing the only thing Hank could do right.

CHAPTER

3

Mrs. D. was waiting outside Room 211.

"How was recess?" she asked.

"Great!" said Maggie. She stuffed some candy wrappers back into her lunch bag. "Sam is really funny, even if his name *is* too hard."

"But Hank is funnier," Sara told her teacher.

"He is not!" said Ty.

"Is too!" said Patrick.

Swish-thump. Swish-thump.

"Come on, now," said Mrs. D. "What's all this arguing? Let's get ready for our health lesson."

Annette raised her hand. "Can Sam tell us about himself first?" she asked. "Where he's from and everything?"

"That's a good idea, Annette," Mrs. D. agreed.

Sam marched to the front of the room.

He stood very straight.

He cleared his throat.

"My full name is Samuel Steven Saurornithoides."

He grinned at Annette and Maggie.

"But as you know, you can call me—"

"DINO-MITE!" they shouted.

"Give me a break," muttered Hank.

"I've lived almost everywhere," Sam continued. "Cave City, Bone Beach,

Fossiltown. Mom and Dad are both astronomers. They study space. They're keeping track of a comet, and they need to watch it from a lot of different places."

"Don't you mind moving around so much?" asked Diana.

"No way! I'd hate to stay in one place a long time. That would be too boring."

Hank sat up straighter. Maybe there *was* hope!

"But Mom and Dad think we'll be here at least a year," Sam finished.

Hank slumped back down.

A whole year!

"Thank you, Sam," said Mrs. D. "We're glad to have you in our class. We hope you'll be here a long time."

Everyone clapped. Everyone but Hank.

Hank gave the spinner on his hat an extra hard flick.

Mrs. D. moved to the front of the room. She pulled down a chart above the chalkboard.

It showed a dinosaur skeleton.

"Today, we're going to talk about bones," she said. "We must all eat the right foods to keep them healthy. Can anyone tell me some good foods for healthy bones?"

"Milk," offered Sara.

"Good, Sara. Growing dinosaurs should drink ten gallons of milk a day. Other ideas?"

"Meat," snarled Rex. "Tons of red, raw meat."

"Yes, for some dinosaurs, like you, Rex, meat is very important."

"Vegetables are wimp food!"

"No, Rex, plants and vegetables

are important for other kinds of dinosaurs."

"Yeah. The sissy kinds."

Mrs. D. went on. "Anyone else want to tell me what we should eat for healthy bones?"

"Chocolate!" Maggie said. Everyone laughed.

Hank couldn't resist. "No, bone-illa!"

Everyone groaned.

Sam raised his hand.

"Bone-anas?" he called.

Swish-thump. Swish-thump.

Mrs. D.'s smile was just about gone.

"Let's get serious, class," she said. "Most of you need fifty or sixty pounds of vegetables every day."

"Who knows what you get when an apatosaurus walks in a vegetable garden?" Sam called out.

"Squash!" yelled Hank.

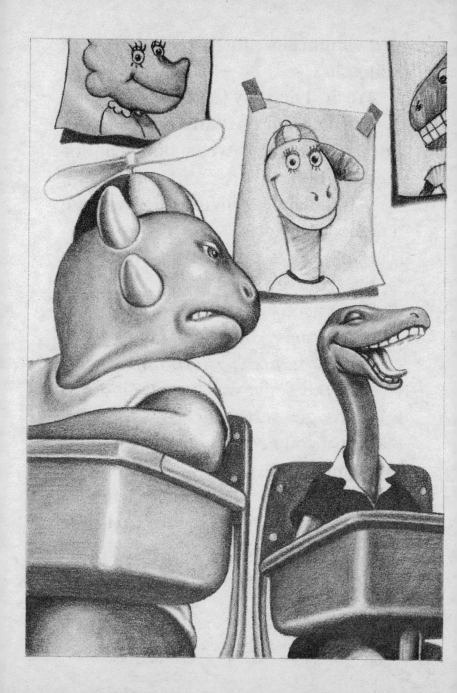

"No, mashed potatoes!" Sam yelled back.

The dinos were almost falling off their chairs. The room was shaking from their laughter.

Mrs. D. rolled the chart back up again. SNAP!

She shook her head. "I see we have *two* comedians now. Lucky us!"

She glanced at the clock.

"It's lunchtime. Maybe some food will put everyone in a more serious mood."

Maggie was already at the door. Her huge lunch bag dragged on the floor behind her. The other dinos jumped out of their chairs.

Swish-thump!

"Walk!" said Mrs. D. "And please, when you come back, let's try to get a *little* work done between jokes."

CHAPTER
4

The Dino School cafeteria was a busy place.

At a table by himself, Rex was shoveling stacks of roast beef sandwiches into his mouth. He swallowed them whole, one after another. His jagged teeth flashed when he opened his mouth.

Annette and Sara and some other girl dinos were eating at their usual table. They were talking about Sara's sleepover on Friday.

"Everyone should bring their Barbiesaurus dolls," Sara told them. "The dolls will have a party, too!"

"Oh, goodie!" said Annette. "Grandma just made my Barbiesaurus a new dress."

"What color?" Maggie wanted to know.

Annette took a handful of potato chips.

"Yellow," she answered. "It looks beautiful with her green skin."

Maggie had just eaten a dozen sandwiches and seven bags of corn crisps. Now she was happily unwrapping a Crunchum bar.

"*My* Barbiesaurus came with makeup and lotion," she said. "It keeps her scales nice and soft."

At the next table, Patrick was on his fourteenth peanut butter sandwich.

Spike was coring apples for Ty with the spikes on his tail.

Little Sam was nibbling carrot sticks from a little bag.

Hank was eating whole tomatoes.

He liked the way they squirted when he bit down.

He picked one up to toss into his mouth.

Then he stopped. He looked at it thoughtfully.

He glanced at Sam.

Sam's mouth was full of carrots.

Fantastic! thought Hank. *Now's my chance.*

"Hey, Patrick," he said. "Know why the tomato blushed?"

He didn't wait for an answer.

"Because he saw the salad dressing!"

Ty drained his gallon of milk.

"That's pretty old, Tank," he said.

"It sure is," agreed Annette. "Like, from the Stone Age."

Hank ignored them. "Come on," he said to Sam. "You know you can't *beet* my vegetable jokes. Ha, ha, ha!"

Ty poked Sam.

"Go ahead, Dino-Mite. Tell a joke!"

Sam swallowed the rest of his carrots. Then he grinned.

"Maybe I don't *carrot* all!"

Hank was quick.

"Well, maybe you should go back where you came from and *lettuce* alone."

Sam was quick, too. And he had a zinger.

"When it comes to jokes, you're nothing but a has-*bean*!"

By now dinos from other tables had

gathered around. Everyone was watching Sam and Hank. Everyone was laughing and clapping.

Annette and Ty were behind Sam.

Maggie joined them. So did Diana.

"I'm definitely on Sam's side," she said happily. "We Dino-Mites need to stick together!"

Sara and Patrick were behind Hank.

Spike was there, too. He wiped off the supercool sunglasses he always wore. Then he picked up Patrick's empty lunch bag.

Hank the Tank, he wrote on one side. He made a number 3 under the name.

Dino-Mite, he wrote on the other side. He made a number 2.

"The Tank is ahead," he announced.

"Not for long," said Sam. He cleared his throat.

"Did you hear about the stegosaurus who went out to eat? He brought his own plates!"

Hank was ready. "What happens when a monster dino goes to a dance? Tyrannosaurus Rocks!"

Rex heard his name. Or something like it.

He came pounding over. "Who's talking about me?" he demanded.

For once no one paid any attention to him.

Everyone was too busy laughing and cheering.

Spike crossed out the old scores. He wrote a 4 and a 3 instead.

"Hank's still in first place," Patrick said happily.

Just then Mrs. D. came over. "What's going on?" she asked.

"They're seeing who can tell the

most jokes," explained Sara. "And Hank is ahead, because he's funnier."

"He is not funnier," Annette objected. "Dino-Mite will catch up fast."

"Oh yeah?"

"Yeah!"

Sara scowled. "Well, anyone who thinks Sam is so funny can forget about coming to my sleepover."

Annette was fuming. "Fine with me. I didn't want to come anyway."

Sara looked at Maggie. She was still behind Sam.

"Well?" Sara asked. She tapped her foot.

"Uh, I *do* think Sam is kind of funny—" Maggie began.

"We're going to have pizza at the sleepover," reminded Sara. "Tons of pizza. Then hot fudge sundaes. Mom's ordered gallons of ice cream already. And for breakfast she's making chocolate chip pancakes in dino shapes."

Maggie looked at Annette and Ty. Their foreheads were wrinkled. They were frowning at her.

"Come on, Maggie," said Ty. "You're not going to change sides because of a little food, are you?"

Maggie crammed her last Crunchum bar into her mouth.

"Of course not," she told him. "Not for a little food."

Then she went over and joined Sara and Patrick.

"But for a *lot* of food? That's different!"

"Now, now," Mrs. D. said. "I think everyone's getting a bit carried away. Is it really necessary to take sides?"

Ty was scowling at his sister. "It sure is," he said. "This is war!"

Sara scowled back at him. "At least a battle," she said.

"Right," said Annette. "The battle of the class clowns!"

Mrs. D. sighed. "Well, how about calling a truce? It's time to get back to our room."

The dinos started to scatter.

Spike picked up the paper bag. He looked at the scores.

"To be continued," he said.

CHAPTER

5

The battle of the class clowns did continue. It continued all afternoon.

Mrs. D. kept trying to teach. But no matter what the lesson was, Sam or Hank made a joke. Spike had to keep changing the score.

Mrs. D. tried a math lesson.

"Iggie Iguanodon weighed three tons when he was two. When he was grown he weighed ten times that much. How many pounds is that?"

"Why don't you check his scales?" asked Hank.

Spike changed the score on the bag.

Mrs. D. tried a lesson on weather.

"Sometimes moisture in the air makes rain. When it's colder we get ice or snow."

Sam chimed in. "And if it were snowing dinosaurs, we'd have a lizard blizzard!"

Spike sharpened his pencil on a spike. He changed the score again.

Mrs. Spinosaurus came in. She was the music teacher. She passed out some songbooks.

Now both dinos got into the act.

First Hank asked, "What do you call a dinosaur who loves to sing? A chorusaurus!"

Then Sam did a knock-knock joke with Annette.

"Knock, knock."

"Who's there?"

"Fossil."

"Fossil who?"

Sam started singing a scale.

"Fos, sil, la, ti, do!"

Spike made two new numbers on the bag. "Tie!" he called out.

"What?" asked Ty.

"Not you, man. I meant, it's a tie score."

"And it's going to stay that way," said Mrs. D.

She marched Hank and Sam down to the principal's office.

"I need help, Ms. Brachiosaurus," she said. "My class simply *must* get some work done this afternoon. We have reading groups. We have science to do. At this rate we'll be here until midnight. Take these two—please!"

"Of course," said the principal. For a minute Hank thought she was going to smile. Then she put on a frown instead.

"Boys, there's a time and place for everything, including jokes. And all day in school is not the place. Do you understand?"

Hank and Sam nodded.

"Now, sit quietly and think serious thoughts for a while. I have lots of work to do myself."

She sharpened a pencil and sat down behind her desk.

The two dinos sat quietly.

For a minute.

For five minutes.

Then it started.

"Uh, Ms. Brachiosaurus?" Sam said.

His voice sounded innocent and sweet.

The principal looked up. She was holding the pencil between her fingers.

"Yes, Sam?"

"What do you do if your car is traveling too fast?"

"Put on the brake-iosaurus!" Hank shouted.

"Hey, that was my joke!" Sam protested.

"Well, you've been stealing mine all day!"

The principal held her pencil tighter. "All right, boys," she said. "I thought we had an agreement about sitting *quietly*."

They looked at each other furiously. Each folded his arms and slumped back.

Ms. Brachiosaurus went back to work. She wrote two paragraphs.

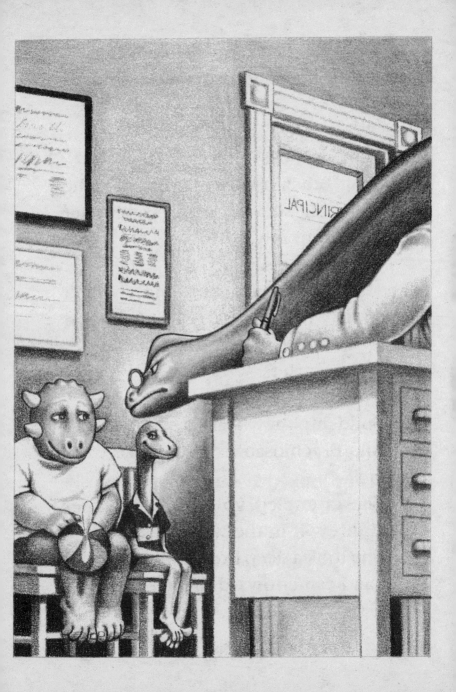

Then she heard Sam's high voice.

"What do ankylosaurs wear on their feet?"

"Who cares?" asked Hank.

"Ankylosocks!" Sam cried.

Ms. Brachiosaurus groaned. She made a big scrawl on her paper. Her concentration was broken.

"Boys!" she said.

Hank started laughing. He couldn't help it. "And when girl ankylosaurs get all dressed up they wear . . . ankylobracelets!"

The dinos laughed and laughed.

Suddenly they heard a sharp crack.

Ms. Brachiosaurus had broken her pencil.

She crumpled up a piece of paper and threw it in the wastebasket.

She took a deep breath. Then she got up and came toward them.

They stopped laughing.

"Hank, sit over there. In the corner, near the window."

Meekly he took a chair across the room.

"Sam, you stay here. Now, not another sound. Not one more word or one more giggle. Do you understand?"

They both nodded.

She sat down again. She picked up a fresh pencil.

She finished her letter.

She began another letter.

Sam and Hank were quiet as mice.

She smiled. She made some notes on her calendar. She neatened her desk.

The dinos were being as good as gold.

"Ready to behave?" she asked them.

They nodded eagerly.

"All right. Let's go back to class."

When she opened the door to Room 211, there were loud cheers.

"Hey, Hank the Tank!" yelled Sara and Patrick.

Sara poked Maggie.

"Yay, Hank!" Maggie called out.

"Way to go, Dino-Mite!" yelled Annette and Ty.

"Sam's our man!" Diana called out.

Everyone clapped and whistled and stomped. Erasers bounced on the chalk tray. Windows rattled.

A classful of happy dinos could really shake a place up.

Even Rex clapped his clawed hands. He slapped Tommy Tarbosaurus's back with his fists.

"Ouch!" Tommy yelled.

Mrs. D. tried to smile. "Back so soon?" she asked.

"They were the very picture of good manners," Ms. Brachiosaurus answered. She smiled at Hank.

"Picture?" said Hank. "How could there be a picture—"

"Without a camarasaurus!" Sam finished.

The class broke up.

"I'll be running along now," said Ms. Brachiosaurus.

She left quickly.

Spike added one more to each score on Patrick's bag.

The score was still tied.

Hank the Tank, 19.

Dino-Mite, 19.

"We should get some credit for the ones in the principal's office," Sam objected.

Spike shook his head. "No, man. I have to hear 'em to count 'em."

"I know!" said Sara. "Let's finish after school."

"On the playground," agreed Annette. "There's some time before the buses leave."

"You're on!" said Hank.

"All right with Dino-Mite!" said Sam.

Mrs. D. broke in. "*Now* maybe we can get back to work. It's time for reading groups. Sam, sit with any group you want today—except Hank's. You two are forbidden to come near each other the rest of the day."

Hank twirled his spinner happily.

He couldn't wait to win the battle.

He had to admit, though, Sam was pretty funny. He remembered Sam's joke from Ms. Brachiosaurus's office. *Ankylosocks*, he thought. Not bad. Sam wasn't as funny as the fabulous Hank the Tank, of course. But he wasn't bad for a beginner.

Oh, well. Dino-Mite would soon be blown away!

CHAPTER
6

Finally school was over. Mrs. D.'s class poured into the hall and then out onto the playground.

They ran over and sat in the bleachers.

Sam and Hank stood at the bottom, facing each other.

Spike stood next to them. He held up the paper bag. It was full of crossouts.

Luckily it was a lunch bag specially made for an apatosaurus. It was enormous.

There was still plenty of room.

"Listen up, guys," said Spike. "Here are the rules. First, anyone in the bleachers can ask a question."

"Or just say a word," Annette put in.

"And then you both have to make jokes about it," finished Sara.

"Ready?" called Spike.

He raised his tail.

"Set!"

The tail was halfway down.

"Go!"

The tail clunked down on the ground.

"I get the first question!" cried Maggie. "Where do dinosaurs eat?"

"At the all-night dino!" yelled Hank.

"In the dino room!" yelled Sam.

Spike made two more crossouts and wrote two more numbers.

"What's a dinosaur's favorite story?" called Diana.

"Allosaurus in Wonderland," said Hank.

"The Lizard of Oz," said Sam.

"Favorite musical instrument?" yelled Sara.

"Trombone!"

"Horns!"

More crossouts. More new numbers.

"I have a question!" called Patrick. "Why did the scaredy-cat dinosaur cross the road?"

Hank and Sam ignored him. They were still going strong on a dinosaur's favorite things. They weren't waiting for the audience.

First Hank. "Favorite toy? A triceratop!"

Then Sam. "Favorite breakfast cereal? Tyrannosaurus Chex!"

Hank started laughing. It was too hard not to.

The dinos in the bleachers were not laughing. They were angry.

"Wait a minute!"

"No fair!"

"*We* get to ask the questions, not you!"

But Hank and Sam paid no attention.

Hank spoke through his laughter. "Favorite music? Playing the scales!"

Sam started laughing, too. "Pretty good," he said. "Favorite dessert? Dino-S'mores!"

Annette stamped her foot. "This is boring," she said angrily.

"I agree," said Sara. She looked at her friend. "I didn't really mean it about the sleepover. Will you come? Please?

It won't be any fun without you."

"Sure," Annette said happily. "I wouldn't miss one of your sleepovers for anything. Especially not for the two class clowns. Let's go wait for the bus."

The two friends slipped off the bleachers.

Diana was practicing gymnastics. She did a neat backflip onto the ground. Then she ran to join Sara and Annette.

Hank and Sam didn't even notice.

They were a team now.

"What do dinosaurs do before they take a test?" Sam asked Hank.

"They bone up!" Hank answered.

The two dissolved in laughter again.

Ty stretched and yawned. "This is as much fun as watching ice cubes freeze," he said to Spike. "Let's go play Heads and Tailsies."

"You're on," said Spike.

Spike left the marked-up, messed-up scorebag on the ground.

But it didn't matter. The class clowns no longer cared about keeping score.

They were having too much fun.

"Where do dinosaurs shop?" asked Sam.

"At the dino-store!" Hank answered. "My turn. What do you call two flying dinosaurs?"

"A pair-a-dactyls!"

They were howling with laughter now.

Maggie and Patrick were practically the only dinos left in the audience.

Maggie finished the box of pretzels she'd been munching. "I have another box in my locker," she told Patrick. "Want to come get it with me?"

Patrick sighed. "Okay. But I wish they would answer my question. I heard it on the radio, but I didn't hear the answer."

Maggie glanced down at Hank and Sam.

They were in a world of their own.

"What do dinosaurs put on the wall in their bathrooms?"

"Rep-tile!"

"Well, I wouldn't hold my breath, if I were you," she told Patrick. "Come on."

Soon the bleachers were completely empty. Dinos were getting on their buses.

Sam and Hank were laughing so hard they had to gasp for breath. They held onto each other. There were tears in their eyes.

Finally they plunked themselves

down on the bottom bleacher.

"Just one more," panted Sam.

"No! Please! I can't take it!" Hank begged.

"I'm sorry. I just have to," Sam said. He took a couple of deep breaths. "What would you say if you saw a hundred dinosaurs on a trampoline?"

They grinned at each other. Then together they shouted, "Leaping Lizards!"

They laughed some more. Then they leaned back, tired and happy.

Suddenly Hank looked up behind him. The bleachers were empty.

"Everyone's gone!" he cried.

Sam turned to the driveway.

"And so are the buses," he exclaimed. "What am I going to do? There's nobody home to pick me up."

The little dino looked worried.

Hank felt sorry for him.

"Come to my house," he said. "It's close. You can wait there until someone's home."

They headed across the grass. Both were quiet for the first time all day.

Then Sam spoke up.

"It doesn't really bother you when someone else tells jokes, does it?"

Hank took off his hat. He watched as the wind made the spinner turn.

"I guess not," he said. "Well, maybe it does. A little."

He put the hat back on.

"It's just that telling jokes is about the only thing I'm good at."

Sam looked surprised. "No way! You're a terrific Heads and Tailsies player, for one thing. And you're good at being a friend. I mean, you must be. You have so many."

Hank thought of Patrick and Sara and Spike. Even Ty and Annette.

Sam was right. They were his friends. And Maggie and Diana, most of the time.

Sam's head was drooping. "My family moves around so much that I don't get a chance to make friends."

"But you said you liked moving around," Hank said.

"I know, but I didn't mean it. I don't mind as much as I used to. At first every time I went to a new school the other dinos laughed at me because of my size. I figured out that I should make them laugh first. That's when I became Dino-Mite, the joke-teller."

The two dinos walked on quietly in the sunshine.

They made two shadows. One was short and thin. One was tall and thick.

All at once there was a third shadow.

They saw it at the same time they heard whirring wheels. Bicycle wheels.

"Oh, no," said Hank. "It's Rex!"

Rex zoomed around them on his big black bike.

He made a double loop, then skidded to a stop. He stood straddling the bike, blocking their path.

"Where's the joke show?" he snarled.

"You're too late, Rex," Hank answered. "It's all over."

"Whaddya mean, it's over? Without me?"

"Right," Sam piped up. "You missed it."

Rex narrowed his eyes. "I missed it, huh? Then I guess I get my own show. Right now. And the jokes better be good, or you guys won't be laughing for a long time!"

Hank sighed. He was too tired to be scared.

"Look, Rex," he tried to explain. "Sam and I are all joked out. We're tired."

"Yes," Sam agreed. "Tired and run down."

Rex put on his nastiest smile.

"Run down? Try this for run down!"

He leaped on the bike and pointed it at them.

"Look out!" Hank called. He pushed Sam behind him. Then he tried to jump out of the way.

He wasn't quick enough. The bike rammed into his side. But it just bounced off Hank's thick, armored skin.

Sam was safe.

Rex went sprawling. His beloved bike wobbled off and hit a tree. Smack!

Hank backed away. "Hey, Sam," he said. "What does a mean, ugly dinosaur do when he gets mad?"

"Anything he wants!" Sam yelled. "Let's get out of here!"

They dashed all the way to Hank's house. They stumbled up onto the porch and inside.

They sat on the living room floor, panting.

"You saved me," Sam said between gasps. "Thanks. Uh, I mean, 'Tanks.'"

Hank grinned at his new friend. It was going to be great having two class clowns.

CHAPTER

7

When the dinos came into Mrs. D.'s class the next day, they were surprised.

Their teacher was wearing lots of necklaces, as usual. Today they were sparkly silver ones.

But she was also wearing earmuffs.

"I can't listen to those dino-jokesters another day," she shouted. "This is just self-protection."

Hank and Sam came into the room together.

Sam seemed to be telling Hank something important.

They weren't laughing. They weren't joking. They weren't even smiling.

They looked very serious as they sat down.

Their classmates waited and watched.

So did Mrs. D.

After a minute she removed the earmuffs.

Sam raised his hand.

"Mrs. D., I have something to say."

Quickly she put the earmuffs back on.

"No, it's not a joke," Sam said. "Really."

He walked to the front of the room.

"Last night Mom and Dad said we're not going to stay," he told the class.

"They can't see the comet very well from here after all. We have to go to Volcanoburg. There's a giant telescope there."

All the dinos were quiet.

They were waiting for a joke.

But Sam looked sad. So did Hank.

There wasn't any joke.

"Oh, Sam, I'm so sorry," said Mrs. D. "We'll miss you. Even the jokes."

Patrick nudged Hank. "That's too bad, but now you'll be the only funny one again."

"Right," said Hank. He stared down at his desk.

"Why do you look so sad, Hank?" asked Sara.

"I don't know. He's . . . he's not a bad guy, you know."

Suddenly Hank waved his hand at Sam.

"Uh, will you write to us, Sam?"

The little dino's face became happy. "Sure," he said.

"And send us some jokes?" Hank continued. "I need some new material every once in a while."

"You got it!"

Patrick raised his hand. "I'm sorry you're leaving, Sam, but before you go, why *did* the scaredy-cat dinosaur cross the road?"

Sam and Hank spoke at the same time. "Because he was really a chicken!"

The other dinos shook with laughter. They bounced up and down. The overhead lights rattled. Chalk and erasers danced on the tray. The water in the fish tank sloshed on the floor.

"Leaping Lizards!" cried Mrs. D.

A few weeks later, Hank took out a sharp pencil.

Dear Sam, he wrote in cursive.

My D is looking better, he thought. *All right!*

The S wasn't so great, though.

All of a sudden, he knew just what to do.

He crossed out Dear Sam.

He started again.

Dear Dino-Mite, he wrote.

Be sure to read the next Dino School book,
Sneeze-O-Saurus.